Jonathan Thayer Lincoln

The Factory

in large print

Jonathan Thayer Lincoln

The Factory

in large print

Reproduction of the original.

1st Edition 2023 | ISBN: 978-3-38730-988-1

Megali Verlag is an imprint of Outlook Verlagsgesellschaft mbH.

Verlag (Publisher): Outlook Verlag GmbH, Zeilweg 44, 60439 Frankfurt, Deutschland
Vertretungsberechtigt (Authorized to represent): E. Roepke, Zeilweg 44, 60439 Frankfurt, Deutschland
Druck (Print): Books on Demand GmbH, In de Tarpen 42, 22848 Norderstedt, Deutschland

THE FACTORY

BY

JONATHAN THAYER LINCOLN

1912

TO MY FATHER

NOTE

This essay is based upon a course of lectures delivered before the Amos Tuck School of Administration and Finance associated with Dartmouth College. These lectures were subsequently printed in *The Mediator*, a magazine published in Cleveland, Ohio, and devoted to establishing a better social understanding between the man who buys and the man who sells labor.

BIBLIOGRAPHICAL NOTE

In preparing the historical part of this essay I have consulted many authorities, and in particular I have made free use of the following works.

DEFOE, Daniel

A plan for the English Commerce, London, 1728.

BAINES, Edward

History of the Cotton Manufacture in Great Britain. London, 1835.

GUEST, Richard

A Compendious History of the Cotton Manufacture. Manchester, 1823.

The Theory and Practice of Cotton Spinning. Glasgow, 1833.

URE, Andrew, M.D.

The Philosophy of Manufactures. London, 1835.

BABBAGE, Charles

On the Economy of Machinery and Manufactures. London, 1822.

CARLYLE, Thomas

Essay on Chartism.

TAYLOR, Richard Whately Cooke-

The Modern Factory System. London, 1891.

ABRAM, Annie

Social England in the Fifteenth Century. London, 1909.

Among the many articles printed in the periodical press the following from the *Quarterly Review* are especially helpful.

Vol. XLI, 1829. Condition of the English Peasantry.

Vol. LVII, 1836. The Factory System.

Vol. LXVII, 1841. Infant Labour.

INTRODUCTION

As you approach the City of the Dinner Pail from the west, the blue waters of the harbor lie between you and the towering factories which line the opposite shore. By day the factories are not attractive to the eye, their massive granite walls, prison-like and unlovely, suggest only the sordid side of toil,—the long day's confinement of twenty-seven thousand men and women amidst the monotonous roar of grinding wheels. But should you thus approach the city late on a winter afternoon the scene is marvelously changed; the myriad lights of the factories shine through the early darkness, transforming prison-walls into fairy palaces, castles of enchantment reflected with mysterious beauty in the deep waters of the bay. There is no suggestion now of sordid toil, the factory walls have become ramparts of light and speak of some romantic story.

Realism and romance lie very near together, and we shall find the factory, when we come to study the history of it, something more than granite walls and grinding machinery; the factory, indeed, has been an important instrument in the upward progress of mankind. There is an ugly side to the story, especially in the beginning, for when the craftsmen of the world were transformed into factory operatives, thousands suffered a degree of poverty never known before, and many perished in the transition to the new system of manufacturing; but in the end that system revolutionized the whole social order, gave to toil its rightful dignity, and, creating a new loyalty to the cause of labor, became an element in the development of modern democracy. It is this brighter side of the story that we have now to consider.

THE FACTORY

I
THE INDUSTRIAL
REVOLUTION

In the fifteenth century the wealth of England, which until then had been made up chiefly of raw products, was greatly increased by the introduction of manufactures, the most important being the making of cloth. Previous to this first extension of industry, it had been impossible for the toiler to rise out of his class except by becoming a priest or a soldier; but with the increase of manufactures wealth became a means of social advancement, and thus industry not only tended to break down the feudal order by tempting serfs away from their masters, but the wealth created by manufactures became an important element in the creation of the middle class.

The sudden and extensive introduction of machinery at the close of the eighteenth century drove hand labor out of employment, and, for a time, caused great suffering among the masses; but in the end it created an ever increasing demand for labor—a new labor more skillful than the old.

Moreover, it concentrated the laboring population in great centres of industry, thus creating a class consciousness which demanded that attention should be given to the rights of labor, created a new ideal of the dignity of toil and gave to the world that vision of the inclusive cause of labor which was destined to advance in a marvelous way to the social progress of mankind.

Slavery had been abolished in England long before the Industrial Revolution, and yet, in the first quarter of the last century men in chains worked in the British coal-mines and were bought and sold when the property changed hands. For generations before the Industrial Revolution, the lord of the manor had ceased to demand the labor of the villein as his due, but while serfdom had been abolished, the traditions of it still remained; and it was not until the establishment of the factory that labor became free in fact as for generations it had been in name.

The historical event, that great movement which led in our generation to a complete reconstruction of the social order, we call the "Industrial Revolution of the Eighteenth Century." It was an extremely complex event, originating in economic, political, and social conditions; but while it was the consequence of many causes, it derived its chief influence in the beginning from a series of remarkable inventions in the art of making textile fabrics.

This art is as old as civilization, originating when men, advancing from barbarism, put aside the skins of beasts for raiment of their own making; but from the days of the first rude distaff and the simple bamboo loom until the time so recently past when, by a series of the most brilliant inventions known to any craft, the art was revolutionized, the implements remained unchanged. Up to the year 1769 the machines in use in the manufacture of cotton cloth in England were practically the same as those which for centuries had been employed in India. There were no factories as there are to-day: the cotton was spun and woven into cloth by hand, and both the spinning and the weaving were done in the cottages of the craftsmen.

The first of these inventions was a simple one, but it made necessary all that followed. From the beginning of the art, one man could weave into cloth all the yarn that several spinners could produce. Indeed, it was seldom that a weaver's family, his wife and children all working at the spinning wheel, could supply sufficient weft for his loom; and this difficulty was increased by the invention of the fly-shuttle in the year 1738. This invention, made by John Kay, consisted in giving motion to the shuttle by a mechanical device which saved time and exertion to the weaver and nearly doubled the daily product of his loom. The increased demand for yarn led to many experiments, and at last a machine was produced upon which many threads could be spun by a single pair of hands: the water frame commonly attributed to Richard Arkwright. With this important invention came many others in the same field, making famous the names of Hargreaves, Crompton, and Cartwright.

The moment it became possible to accomplish by machinery what formerly had been done entirely by hand, the first effect was to increase the productive power of the workman and thus to add vastly to the wealth of the nation, and secondly, to gather into the factories the craftsmen who had formerly worked in their homes.

In the beginning of the eighteenth century the textile manufacturing of England was carried on by craftsmen dwelling in the rural districts, the master clothiers living in the greater towns, sending out wool to be spun into yarn which, returned to them prepared for the loom, was re-distributed among other hand workers in other cottages. The Lancashire weaver worked in his cottage surrounded by a bit of land, and generally combined small farming with domestic manufacturing. Sometimes a single family performed all the labor, the wife and daughters working at carding and spinning, the father operating the loom; sometimes other craftsmen joined the household and worked as members of one family. The extent of mercantile establishments and the modes of doing business were very different from what they were soon to become. It is quite true that a limited number of individuals had, in previous ages, made fortunes by trade, but until the very end of the seventeenth century the capital in the hands of British merchants was small. Because of the bad condition of the roads and the lack of inland navigation, goods were conveyed by pack horses with which the Manchester chapmen traveled through the principal towns, selling their goods to the shopkeepers, or at the public fairs, and bringing back sheep's wool to be sold to the clothiers of the manufacturing districts.

In the writings of modern socialists we find the domestic system held up for admiration as the ideal method of production. The dreamers look back regretfully to the days when manufactures were combined with farming, and they quote from Goldsmith's *Deserted Village*. Let us, however, turn to a more prosaic but more trustworthy account, which is to be found in Daniel Defoe's *Plan of the English Commerce*. The author is writing enthusiastically in praise of English manufactures, and, having pointed out how in the unemployed counties women and children are seen idle and out of business, the women sitting at their doors, the children playing in the street, he continues: "Whereas, in the manufacturing counties, you see the wheel going almost at every door, the wool and yarn hanging up at every window;

the looms, the winders, the combers, the carders, the dyers, the dressers all busy; and the very children as well as the women constantly employed ... indeed there is not a poor child in the town above the age of four but can earn his own bread."

When we come to study the brutalizing social conditions which obtained in the manufacturing towns following the establishment of the factory, we shall do well to keep in mind these words written by an eighteenth century student in praise of the domestic system; when we hear the socialists declare that the factory created wage slavery, let us remember this earlier and more monstrous slavery.

Richard Arkwright, the inventor of the spinning-frame, was a man of great genius. Endowed with the inventive faculty, and even more with the ability to perfect the inventions of others, he possessed as well extraordinary executive ability, and having brought his spinning machinery to the point of practical efficiency, he organized the modern factory system as the means of obtaining the highest results from the new mechanisms. The spinning frame was too cumbersome to be operated in the cottage, and, moreover, it required a greater power to operate it than that of the human hand, so Arkwright built his first factory which was run by horse power, and from this beginning was evolved the factory as we know it to-day. But important as were the inventions in cotton manufacture, the factory would never have become the mighty power that it is, except for the steam engine; and it is interesting to note that in the same year in which Arkwright took out his patent for spinning by rollers, Watt invented his device for lessening the consumption of fuel in fire engines, that epoch-making invention by means of which the factory system as perfected by Arkwright was to become the material basis of modern life.

Like the Renaissance, the Industrial Revolution was a movement destined to change the very course of human thought. Mechanical invention contributed to the force of the earlier movement—the invention of printing and of the mariner's compass—so that side by side with the scholars restoring to the world its lost heritage of learning, craftsmen and sailors played their parts in printing the books by which the learning was disseminated, and in manning the ships that discovered new continents. The Renaissance, however, was essentially an intellectual movement to which mechanical invention was merely an aid, while the Industrial Revolution was due in an important measure to machinery. The movement began in the cotton industry, but soon a similar expansion occurred in all other manufactures. Machinery made possible a vast production; and the steam engine, first applied to manufacture, later became the means of distributing the commodities.

The Industrial Revolution, thus springing from the sudden growth in the use of machinery, occasioned not only economic but political and social results. On the economic side, the effect was to extend old industries and to create new ones, as well as to revolutionize the methods of the production and distribution of wealth. On the social side it created new classes of men, breaking down the barriers of ancient feudalism, and on the political side it led to the enfranchisement of the working classes. The Industrial Revolution accomplished for England what the political revolution did for France, but by more peaceful means. Yet not alone in France was the event achieved in blood—for the Factory as well as the Terror had its victims. The history of the factory is no dry summary of patent rights and inventions, inventories of cotton and cotton goods, abstracts of ledgers, journals, cash-books, and pay-rolls,—it is a human story,—*laissez-faire*, over-production, enlightened selfishness, were no abstract terms, but vital human problems.

Because the Industrial Revolution profoundly influenced the social and political life of England, and later of the whole world, the history of the factory, which contributed so much to its influence, becomes of vast importance. The first chapter relates to brilliant achievements in the field of mechanical invention. Then follows the dismal story of how a multitude of craftsmen were transformed into factory operatives—the untold suffering of oppressed workingmen. Later we see the English yeoman replaced by the master manufacturer who soon became a force in the political life of the nation, finding his way into Parliament and even into the Peerage. For the common people the revolution began with great suffering, but ended in opening new avenues for their social and political advancement. Antagonistic in the beginning to the welfare of the masses, it aided powerfully, in the end, the fulfillment of those ideals of liberty, equality, and fraternity which at that moment had taken such a mighty hold upon the thoughts of men.

II
SIR RICHARD ARKWRIGHT

The *Shaving of Shagpat*, that remarkable allegory with the writing of which George Meredith commenced his literary career, has been given several interpretations; without seriously venturing another, it has seemed to me that this fanciful story deals with the chief events in the Industrial Revolution.

"So there was feasting in the hall and in the city, and over earth": we read towards the end of the tale, "great pledging the sovereign of Barbers, who had mastered an event and become the benefactor of his craft and of his kind. 'Tis sure the race of Bagarags endured for many centuries, and his seed were the rulers of men, and the seal of their empire stamped on mighty wax the Tackle of Barbers."

Shibli Bagarag,—could he not well have been Richard Arkwright, the barber, inventor of the spinning-frame, master of an event? In Shagpat the Clothier, we discover the smug and comfortable British aristocracy; in the Identical, that magic hair in Shagpat's beard which gave him a position of power greater even than the King, we observe Feudal Privilege; the sword of Aklis, with the steel of which the Identical was cut, may well stand for the factory, a weapon gained after many trials by Arkwright, so that of him it might be written as it was of Shibli Bagarag: "Thou, even thou will be master of the event, so named in anecdotes, and histories, and records, to all succeeding generations."

Richard Arkwright, who first saw the light of day at Preston on the 23d of December, 1732, was the youngest of thirteen children born to humble parents, and he grew to manhood without education, being barely able to read and write. At an early age he was apprenticed to a Preston barber and when he became a journeyman he established himself in the same business.

Fate was in a jesting mood when she decreed that the chief actor in that remarkable social drama, the Industrial Revolution, should be a penny barber; and we may wonder if the governing classes appreciated the irony, when twenty years later, in recognition of his genius, the barber was raised to the honor of knighthood and his lady privileged to walk before the wives of the untitled gentry.

Richard Arkwright, at the age of twenty-eight, was not content day after day to shave the stolid faces of lower class Englishmen, but, having gained a knowledge of a chemical process for dyeing human hair, he commenced to make wigs for upper class Englishmen—wigs dyed to suit any complexion. This occupation took him away from the barber's chair and sent him traveling about the country. On such a tour in 1761, he met a lady in the city of Leigh,— Margaret Biggins was her name,—and he married her; and in the same city at a somewhat later date he heard of certain experiments which had been made by a man named High in constructing a machine for spinning yarn. He gained this secret from a clock-maker named Kay, with whom he afterwards formed a partnership, by getting Kay—so the gossips said—loquaciously drunk at a public-house. Concerning his wife, history has little to say except that she quarreled with him because of the interest he took in High's machine; and commencing to make experiments on his own account he became so absorbed in his workshop that his lady, fearing that they might be thrown upon the parish for support, begged him to return to his razor, and because he refused smashed the first model of the spinning-machine and thus precipitated a tremendous family row.

Arkwright is commonly credited with the invention of spinning by rollers, but while to him is undoubtedly due the success of that invention he did not originate it. The inventor of that ingenious process was neither Arkwright nor High, but John Wyatt of Birmingham, who in 1738 took out a patent in the name of Lewis Paul. In 1741 or 1742 these two men set up in Birmingham a mill "turned by two asses walking around an axis," and in which ten girls were employed; while later a larger mill containing two hundred and fifty spindles and giving employment to twenty-five operatives was built. Wyatt wrote a pamphlet entitled, *A Systematic Essay on the Business of Spinning*, in which he showed the great profits which would attend the establishment of a plant of three hundred spindles. Wyatt's factory, however, did not prosper and it seems probable that his machinery also passed into the hands of Arkwright.

It was in the year 1767 that Hargreaves invented the spinning-jenny, and two years later Arkwright took out his patent claiming that he had "by great study and long application invented a new piece of machinery, never before found out, practiced or used, for the making of weft or yarn from cotton, flax, and wool; which would be of great utility to a great many manufacturers, as well as to His Majesty's subjects in general, by employing a great number of poor people in working the said machinery and in making the said weft or yarn much superior in quality to any heretofore manufactured or made." However lacking in originality this famous invention may have been, however great may have been the debt which Arkwright owed to Wyatt and Paul, to John Kay and to High, nevertheless, to him belongs all the credit of the first successful introduction of spinning by machinery.

Having obtained this patent, Arkwright found himself without the capital necessary for carrying out his plans; and he returned to his native city of Preston and there applied to a friend, Mr. John Smalley, a liquor merchant, for assistance. So reduced were his circumstances at this time that going to vote at a contested election, which occurred during his visit to Preston, his wardrobe was in so tattered a condition that a number of his friends advanced the money to purchase decent clothes in which he might appear in the poll-room; and once during this period he having applied for pecuniary aid to a Mr. Atherton, that gentleman refused to entertain

Arkwright's plan because of the rags in which the inventor was dressed.

It was in Preston, then, that Arkwright first fitted up his perfected spinning machine, in the parlor of a house belonging to the free grammar school. Here Arkwright successfully demonstrated the utility of his invention and first received financial support. In consequence of the riots which had taken place in the neighborhood of Blackburn on the invention of Hargreaves's spinning-jenny, by which many of the machines were destroyed and the inventor driven from his native county to Nottingham, Arkwright and Smalley, fearing similar outrages, also went to Nottingham accompanied by John Kay, the loquacious clock-maker; so that Nottingham became the cradle of the two great inventions in cotton spinning. Here, Arkwright also applied for aid to the Messrs. Wright, Bankers, who made advances on the condition that they should share in the profits of the invention; but as the machine was not perfected as soon as they had hoped they withdrew their support and he turned to Mr. Samuel Need, a partner of Jedidiah Strutt, the inventor of the stocking frame. Strutt examined Arkwright's mechanism, declared it to be an admirable invention, and the two men of wealth agreed to a partnership with the Preston barber; and a mill was erected at Nottingham.

It was an unpretentious establishment, that first little cotton mill; it gave employment to not more than a dozen operatives, and the machinery was turned not by a great steam engine, but by a pair of patient horses harnessed to a treadmill,—yet it contained the germ of the modern factory and the modern factory system. Later, Arkwright built another and larger factory at Cromford in Derbyshire, driven by water power—from which circumstance his spinning-machine came to be called the water-frame.

The cotton industry of England which Arkwright established developed slowly; in the five years, ending with 1775, the annual import of cotton into Great Britain was only four times the average import at the beginning of the century. But when in the year 1785 Arkwright's patent was finally set aside and his spinning machinery became public property, a great extension of cotton manufacture followed, accompanied by a marvelous national prosperity. Arkwright, although deprived of his monopoly, was by this time so firmly established in the industry that he remained the dominant figure in the yarn market, fixing the price of the commodity for all other spinners; and thus he accumulated a great fortune.

While Arkwright was without doubt perfectly familiar with the experiments of both Wyatt and High, nevertheless it was the Preston barber and not the original inventors who first produced yarn fit for weaving. It is proverbial that inventors seldom reap the harvest of wealth which they sow; they are the dreamers and their reward is in beholding a perfected mechanism—their work of art. So it was with Wyatt and High. They dreamed of spindles turned by power and saw their spindles turn; but Arkwright dreamed of a nation made rich and powerful by these same inventions, and he, too, lived to see his dream come true.

Sir Richard Arkwright possessed all the qualities essential to success—tireless energy, enthusiasm, perseverance, and self-confidence. He believed in himself and so he compelled others to believe in him. His usual working day began at five o'clock in the morning and did not end until nine at night; when he was fifty years of age he lengthened this day by two hours, which he devoted to acquiring the education denied him in his youth. He had unbounded confidence in the success of his adventures and was accustomed to say that he would pay the national debt—an interesting circumstance, for surely by his genius the national debt was paid many times over.

In the year 1786 he was appointed high sheriff of Derbyshire, and when about that time the King narrowly escaped assassination at the hands of Margaret Nicholson, Arkwright, having presented an address of congratulation from his county to the King, received the honor of knighthood. He died on the 3d of August, 1792, at the age of sixty. The *Annual Register* recording that event says not so much as a single word concerning Arkwright's masterful genius which even then had set in motion a mighty social revolution. It mentions only the great fortune which he had acquired as a manufacturer of cotton yarn,—so difficult it is for the critic to place a true value on the life work of a contemporary.

As you approach the City of the Dinner Pail from the west and gaze across the blue waters of the harbor, the eye rests upon the towering factories which line the opposite shore. Within those walls twenty-seven thousand men and women living in a degree of comfort never known before to the spinners and weavers of the world, earn their daily bread. Those towering factories are, every one, monuments to the genius of Richard Arkwright, the penny barber of Preston. If he appropriated the inventions of others, he perfected these inventions and made them of permanent value to mankind; and moreover, he arranged the machinery into series, organized the factory system, and revolutionized industry.

Says Carlyle: "Richard Arkwright, it would seem, was not a beautiful man; no romance hero with haughty eyes, Apollo lip, and gesture like the herald Mercury; a plain, almost gross, bag-cheeked, pot-bellied Lancashire man, with an air of painful reflection, yet also of copious free digestion;—a man stationed by the community to shave certain dusty beards in the northern parts of England at halfpenny each.... Nevertheless, in strapping razors, in lathering of dusty beards, and the contradictions and confusions attendant thereon the man had notions in that rough head of his; spindles, shuttles, wheels and contrivances plying ideally within the same, rather hopeless looking, which, however, he did at last bring to bear. Not without great difficulty! his townsfolk rose in mob against him, for threatening to shorten labor, to shorten wages; so that he had to fly, with broken wash pots, scattered household, and seek refuge elsewhere. Nay, his wife, too, rebelled; burned his wooden model of his spinning wheel; resolute that he should stick to his razors, rather;—for which, however, he decisively, as thou wilt rejoice to understand, packed her out of doors. Oh! reader, what a Historical Phenomenon is that bag-cheeked, pot-bellied, much-enduring, much-inventing barber! French revolutions were a-brewing, to resist the same in any measure, Imperial Kaisers were impotent without the cotton and cloth of England; and it was this man who gave to England the power of cotton."

III
MECHANICAL INVENTIONS

A distinction should be made between the factory and the factory system. The latter was not new to England, having been employed during the Roman occupation; and with the introduction of the woolen industry under Edward III, we again find the factory system established on an extensive scale.

John Winchcombe, commonly called Jack of Newbury, who died about the year 1520, made use of the factory system on a very extensive scale. In Fuller's *Worthies* you may read how he "was the most considerable clothier without fancy or fiction England ever beheld," and how "his looms were his lands, whereof he kept one hundred in his house, each managed by a man and a boy." Jack of Newbury was celebrated in a metrical romance, and the following lines taken from it contain an interesting description of his famous industrial establishment.

"Within one room, being large and long,

There stood two hundred looms full strong:

Two hundred men the truth is so,

Wrought in these looms all in a row;

By every one a pretty boy

Sat making quills with mickle joy.

And in another place hard by

A hundred women merily

Were carding hard with joyful cheer

Who, singing sat with voices clear;

And in a chamber close beside

Two hundred maidens did abide,

These pretty maids did never lin

But in their place all day did spin:

Then to another room came they

Where children were in poor array,

And every one sat picking wool,

The finest from the coarse to cull:

The number was seven score and ten

The children of poor silly men,

Within another place likewise

Full fifty proper men he spied,

And these were sheer men every one,

Whose skill and cunning there was shown:

A dyehouse likewise he had then

Wherein he kept full forty men:

And also in his fulling mill,

Full twenty persons kept he still."

Here, indeed, we have the factory system—in which the division of labor is a conspicuous feature—employed with all its modern details; but not the steam-driven factory, building great cities and changing the whole social life of the kingdom.

The original mode of converting cotton into yarn was by the use of distaff and spindle, a method still employed in the remote parts of India. The distaff is a wooden rod to which a bundle of cotton is tied loosely at one end, and which the spinner holds between the left arm and the body while with his right hand he draws out and twists the cotton into a thread. This simple process is the basis of all the complicated spinning machinery in use at the present time.

In a modern cotton factory there are three departments of labor, carding, spinning, and weaving; and we have now to consider briefly these three processes. The purpose of carding is to clean the cotton and lay the fibres in a uniform direction. This was at first accomplished by hand, the implement employed being little different from an ordinary comb; later an improved device was used consisting of a pair of large wire brushes. This, we must observe, was a primitive operation, and the amount of cotton which one person could thus prepare for spinning was very small.

We have already seen that the invention of the fly-shuttle so increased the demand for yarn that ingenious men were induced to make mechanical experiments for the purpose of supplying this demand—experiments which, in the end, led to the invention of the spinning-frame. The spinning-frame, in turn, increased the demand for carded cotton and skillful mechanics again set about to meet this new requirement, and the result was the building of the carding-engine. This invention was not made at once, nor by any particular individual; but was the result of a number of improvements made at different times and by different persons. One of these men was Thomas High, the inventor of the spinning-jenny; another was James Hargreaves who so improved the jenny that he is commonly called the inventor of it; and finally, Richard Arkwright himself took the crude machine devised by these men and perfected it. Thus it came about that the modern carding-engine as well as the spinning-frame, was made of practical value by this much-enduring, much-inventing barber.

The invention of the fly-shuttle, as we have seen, led to an increased demand for yarn, and this demand was further augmented about the year 1760 when the Manchester merchants began to export cotton goods in considerable quantities to Italy, Germany, and the North American colonies. It was then no uncommon thing for a weaver to walk three or four miles in the morning, and call on five or six spinners, before he could collect yarn enough to serve him for the remainder of the day.

Ingenious mechanics set about the task of producing more yarn. The first of these was Thomas High, a reed maker, residing in the town of Leigh, who engaged one Kay, a clock-maker, and this is the same Kay who was afterwards employed by Arkwright to make the wheels and other apparatus for a spinning-machine. This machine was set up in the garret of High's house. Now, Thomas High had a daughter who watched with keen interest the progress of his experiments—her name was Jane—and in honor of her he called the machine the spinning-jenny. It is commonly stated—even in so authoritative a history as Baines's we find the error—that the credit for the original invention of the spinning-jenny is due to Hargreaves, he having made the first machine in 1767. But Guest has shown quite conclusively by the sworn statement of one Thomas Leather, a neighbor of High, that the latter completed a similar machine in 1764.

However this may be, James Hargreaves, a weaver of Stand-Hill, near Blackburn, perfected the original jenny and made it a practical working machine so that history has quite justly named him the author. From the first Hargreaves was aware of the value of his invention, but not having the ambition to obtain a patent he kept the machine as secret as possible, using it only to spin yarn for his own weaving. An unprotected invention of such importance, however, could not remain long the private property of a single weaver, and soon a knowledge of his achievement spread throughout the neighborhood; but instead of gaining admiration and gratitude for Hargreaves, the spinners raised the cry that the invention would throw multitudes out of employment and a mob broke into his house and destroyed his jenny.

After this, Hargreaves moved to Nottingham, where, with a Mr. Thomas James, he raised sufficient capital to erect a small mill; here he took out a patent in 1770,—one year after Arkwright had patented the water-frame. Before leaving Lancashire, Hargreaves made and sold to other weavers a number of jennies; and in spite of all opposition the importance of the invention led to its general use.

A desperate effort was made in 1779, during a period of distress, to put down the machine. A mob scoured the country for miles around Blackburn demolishing jennies and with them all carding-engines, water-frames, and other machinery; but the rioters spared the jennies which had only twenty spindles, as these were by this time admitted to be useful to the craftsmen. Not only the working classes, but the middle and even the upper classes entertained at this time a profound dread of machinery. The result of these riots was to drive spinners and other capitalists from the neighborhood of Blackburn to Manchester, increasing the importance of that rapidly growing town which was destined to become the world centre of the cotton industry.

The story of this early opposition to the introduction of machinery deserves attention not only as an interesting episode in the history of the factory, but because even to-day a similar opposition comes to the surface with each new improvement in the method of manufacture. It is also an interesting fact that Lord Byron made his maiden speech in the House of Lords in opposition to the Nottingham Riot Bills, introduced into Parliament for the protection of owners of machinery. There were two of these bills, one "for the more exemplary punishment of persons destroying or injurying any stocking- or lace-frames, or other machines or engines used in the frame-work knitting manufactory, or any articles or goods in such frames or machines"; the other "for the more effectual preservation of the peace within the county of Nottingham."

These two bills were the result of rioting among the lacemakers of this county and their object was to increase the penalty for breaking machinery, from transportation to death, to permit the appointment of special constables in times of disturbance, and to establish watch and ward throughout the disturbed parts. These bills and the debates upon them throw a strong light upon the extent of the disturbances, and indicate the attitude of the government, at that time, toward the laboring poor.

The important inventions in carding and spinning led to a rapid advance in cotton manufacture; the new machines not only turned off a greater quantity of yarn than had been produced by hand, but the yarn was also of a superior quality. The water-frame spun a hard, firm yarn, well adapted for warps, while the jenny produced a soft yarn suitable for spinning weft; but the yarn produced on neither of these machines could be advantageously used for making the finer qualities of goods.

This defect in the spinning-machinery was remedied by still another device called the mule jenny, but now termed simply the mule, so named because it combined the principles of both Arkwright's water-frame and Hargreaves' jenny. The mule was invented by Samuel Crompton, a weaver living at Hall-in-the-Wood near Bolton. He commenced his experiments in 1774, but it was five years before he completed the machine. Crompton took out no patent and only regretted that public curiosity would not allow him to keep his little invention for himself. The mule was first known as the Hall-in-the-Wood wheel, then as the muslin wheel because it made yarn sufficiently fine for weaving that fabric, and finally by its present name.

As the inventor made no effort to secure a patent, the mule became public property, and was generally adopted by manufacturers, but Crompton himself received no other reward than a grant of five thousand pounds voted him by Parliament in 1812. Although his means were small, he was always in easy circumstances, until the latter part of his life, when, being no longer able to work, he was reduced to poverty. Certain manufacturers who had profited by his invention then subscribed for the purchase of a life annuity, to which fund foreign as well as English spinners contributed. Crompton died on January 26, 1827.

Having considered the inventions in the art of spinning, we now turn to the power loom built in 1785 by the Reverend Edmund Cartwright, of Hollander House, Kent. A loom moved by water power had been contrived as early as the seventeenth century by one De Gennes, and described as "a new engine to make linen cloth without the help of an artificer." But the machine never came into general use; and in about the middle of the eighteenth century there is record of another power loom, also a French invention, which suffered a similar fate. Describing his own loom Cartwright says that in the summer of 1784 he fell in company with some gentlemen of Manchester who were discussing Arkwright's spinning-machinery. One of the company observed that, as soon as Arkwright's patents expired, so many mills would be erected and so much cotton spun that hands could not be found to weave it.

To this observation the ingenious clergyman replied that Arkwright should set his wits to work to invent a weaving-mill. But the Manchester gentlemen unanimously agreed that the thing was impractical. Cartwright argued, however, that, having seen exhibited in London an automaton figure which played at chess, he did not believe it more difficult to construct a machine which would weave. He kept this conversation in mind and later employed a carpenter and a blacksmith to carry his ideas into effect. Thus he built a loom which, to his own delight, produced a piece of cloth. The machine, however, required two powerful men to work it, but Cartwright, who was entirely unfamiliar with the art of weaving, believed that he had accomplished all that was required, and on the 4th of April, 1785, he secured a patent. It was only then that he commenced to study the method by which the craftsmen wove cloth, and he was astonished when he compared the easy working of the hand loom with his own ponderous engine. Profiting by his study, however, he produced a loom which in its general principles is precisely the same as the looms used to-day.

Thus was invented the machinery of the cotton mill; but there remains to be considered the one other contrivance without which the vast extension of manufactures would have been impossible and the manufacturing towns, which we are about to consider, would never have attained the size and importance which enabled them to become factors in the political life of England. I refer to the steam engine.

In 1763, James Watt was employed in repairing a model of Newcomen's steam engine, and, noting certain basic defects, undertook to remedy them. He perceived the vast possibilities of a properly constructed engine and, after years of patient labor he gave to the world the mighty power of steam. Previous to this time, and indeed until the year 1782, the steam engine had been used almost exclusively to pump water out of mines, but with Watt's improvements it became possible for the engine to give rotary motion to machinery.

The first cotton mill to install a steam engine made by Boulton and Watt was the one owned by the Messrs. Robinson in Nottinghamshire—this was about the year 1785. Two years earlier, Arkwright had made use of an atmospheric engine in his Manchester factory, but it was not until 1789 that an improved steam engine was set up in that city and it was a year later when Arkwright adopted the device.

The invention of spinning-machinery created the cotton manufacture of England, but the industry would never have reached the proportions which it presently did except for the genius of Watt.

IV
THE FACTORY SYSTEM

When the cotton manufacture was in its infancy, all the operations, from dressing the raw material to folding the finished fabric, were completed under the roof of the weaver's cottage. With Arkwright's invention it became the custom to spin the yarn in factories and weave it by hand in cottages. With the invention of the power loom, it again became the practice to perform all the processes in a single building.

The weaver's cottage, then, with its rude apparatus of peg warping, hand cards, spinning-wheels, and wooden looms, was the steam factory in miniature; but the amount of labor performed in a single factory was as great as that which formerly gave occupation to the inhabitants of an entire district. A good hand-loom weaver could produce two pieces of shirtings each week; by 1823, a power-loom weaver produced seven such pieces in the same time.

A factory containing two hundred looms was operated by one hundred persons who wove seven hundred pieces a week, and it was estimated that under the domestic system at least eight hundred and seventy-five looms would have been required to weave this amount of cloth, because the women of the household had their home duties to perform while the men were required to devote a considerable portion of their time to farming. It was therefore further estimated that the work done in a steam factory containing two hundred looms would, if performed by hand, give employment and support to a population of more than two thousand persons. It is interesting here to note, that, whereas a hand-loom weaver could produce two pieces of shirtings a week, an ordinary weaver is now able to turn off eight or ten pieces of equal length every ten hours; so that a modern weave room containing two hundred power looms operated by twenty-five weavers represents the labor of a community of sixty thousand craftsmen, their wives and their children. A population of thirty million would be required to perform by hand the work now produced by the Fall River factories alone.

"Watt," said a celebrated French engineer, "improves the steam engine, and this single improvement causes the industry of England to make an immense stride. This machine, at the present time [about 1830], represents the power of three hundred thousand horses or of two million men, strong and well fitted for labor, who should work night and day without an interruption and without repose.... A hairdresser invents, or at least brings into action, a machine for spinning cotton; this alone gives the British industry immense superiority. Fifty years only, after this great discovery, more than one million of the inhabitants of England are employed in those operations which depend, directly or indirectly, on the action of this machine. Lastly, England exports cotton, spun and woven by an admirable system of machinery, to the value of four hundred million francs yearly.... The British navigator travels in quest of the cotton of India, brings it from a distance of four thousand leagues, commits it to an operation of the machines of Arkwright, carries back their products to the East, making them again to travel four thousand leagues, and in spite of the loss of time—in spite of the enormous expense incurred by this voyage of eight thousand leagues, the cotton manufactured by the machinery of England becomes less costly than the cotton of India, spun and woven by hand near the field that produced it, and sold at the nearest market. So great is the power of the progress of machinery."

Two distinct systems of production preceded the factory. First, the system of isolated handicraft labor, and second, the system of cottage industry, which we have already considered and in which the several members of a family participated,—this, too, was handicraft. The craftsman, as we have seen, worked with his family in his own cottage; he owned his loom and the other simple machinery necessary for the production of cloth, and either he owned his raw material or received it from the master manufacturer to be returned in the form of finished fabric. But in either case, the craftsman was his own master and sold cloth not labor.

With the establishment of the factory, these conditions were completely changed. The master manufacturer not only owned the factory building and the machinery, but he owned the raw material. Moreover to him the operative sold his labor which thereby became a commodity quite as completely as the cotton he wove into cloth. This latter circumstance is important because it became the source of the vast social discontent which, in the end, aided powerfully in revolutionizing the structure of British society.

To the consideration of this event we shall soon return. For the moment we must consider briefly the most characteristic distinction in the process of manufacture under the new system—the extension of the principle of division of labor.

The principle itself was in no wise new, for the first application of it was made in a very early stage in the evolution of society. At the very dawn of civilization it must have become apparent that more comforts and conveniences could be acquired by one man restricting his occupation to a single craft—and the development of independent arts was in itself a division of labor. The same principle was then carried into the different trades, and at last we find it fully developed in the cottage system of industry. Thus we find carding, spinning, and weaving carried on by separate members of the family. Carding and spinning, which required less bodily strength, was performed by the women, while the more laborious work of weaving was given over to the men. With the establishment of the factory and the introduction of machinery, means were supplied by which this system could attain its highest development.

The advantages resulting from the division of labor are evident. When the whole work in any art is executed by one person, that person must possess sufficient skill to perform the most difficult, and sufficient strength to perform the most laborious, of the processes; but by employing a division of labor several persons may be kept at work executing that part of the whole for which he is best fitted.

The further advantages may be most briefly stated in the familiar words of Adam Smith: "The great increase in the quantity of work, which, in consequence of the division of labor, the same number of people are capable of performing, is owing to three different circumstances: first, to the increase of dexterity in every particular workingman; secondly, to the saving of time, which is commonly lost in passing from one species of work to another, and, lastly, to the invention of a great number of machines which facilitate and abridge labor and enable one man to do the work of many."

It should be noted that the factory was, in the beginning, not the creation of capital, but of labor. The early master manufacturers were risen workingmen. Sir Richard Arkwright, the creator of the factory, the man who dominated industrial activities in the first great period of expansion, was a penny barber; but he died a Knight Bachelor with an income greater than that of many a prince.

The process of social elevation by means of trade began back in the fifteenth century with the first extension of manufactures. By the beginning of the eighteenth century it was possible to name five hundred great estates within a hundred miles of London, which, at no remote time, had been possessions of the ancient English gentry, but had later been bought up by tradesmen and manufacturers. The ancestors of these new landed proprietors had been, less than three hundred years before, not soldiers, but serfs.

Moreover, generations before the establishment of the factory, important towns had been raised by manufactures—towns of which Manchester and Birmingham were examples, in which there were few or no families of the gentry, yet which were full of families richer by far than many a noble house. And side by side with this process of tradesmen rising to the gentry had gone the other process of declining gentry placing their sons in trade. So, as Defoe pithily said, "Tradesmen became gentlemen by gentlemen becoming tradesmen."

The successful artisan under the domestic system became in time master clothier, and when the factory became the means of further increase to their fortunes the capital which this class had already amassed was utilized in building mills and machinery. To this class belonged the grandfather of Sir Robert Peel, a resident of Blackburn, who supported himself from the profits of a farm in the neighborhood and devoted his spare time to mechanical experiments. From this he came to operate a print-works, and later commenced the manufacture of cloth.

His son, the first Sir Robert,—the father of the Prime Minister,—was apprenticed to the trade and came to manhood at the time when the impulse given to manufactures in England, through the introduction of machinery, led to a more rapid accumulation of wealth than had been known in any previous period of history. It is said that in his youth Robert Peel entertained a presentiment that he would become the founder of a family. By means of the factory, he amassed a fortune, was raised to the honor of knighthood, and realized his presentiment—for in the next generation no name is more famous in the annals of government than that of Sir Robert Peel, the grandson of a domestic manufacturer.

As the number of factories increased it became possible for operatives to rise, first to positions of trust within the factory, and later to the rank of master manufacturer—so that many a bobbin boy became a cotton lord.

Within the factory the effect was to intensify that spirit of discontent which presently arose among the workers—for risen workingmen are apt to prove the hardest task masters.

A graphic picture of this aspect of factory life as it existed in Manchester in the first half of the last century, when discontent had become articulate and the great Chartist movement reached its height is to be found in Dickens's *Hard Times*. In that story Josiah Bounderby of Coketown is typical of this class of risen workingmen—the early employers of labor under the factory system; Josiah Bounderby, who learnt his letters from the outside of shops and was first able to tell time from studying the steeple clock at St. Giles's Church, London; Josiah Bounderby, vagabond, errand boy, laborer, porter, clerk, chief manager, small partner, merchant, banker, manufacturer. There was very little in the training of Josiah Bounderby, or any of his class to make them humane employers of labor—and among the several causes which made the early relation of employer and employee under the factory system one of bitter strife, this cause, so strictly social in its origin, is one of the most important.

The establishment of the factory altered completely the relation between employer and employee. Indeed in the modern sense these relations were then first established. Labor became a commodity which the master manufacturer, who was also the capitalist, bought and which the workingman sold. When in the year 1785 Arkwright's patents were set aside and the use of his perfected spinning machinery became free to all manufacturers, a great extension of the cotton industry followed. Factories were built throughout Lancashire and about these factories important cities sprang up in which the modern problem of the relation of employer and employee had its beginning.

The factory produced cloth more cheaply and in far greater quantity than was possible under the domestic system. Hand workers sought employment in the factories. Vast numbers of purely agricultural laborers left the rural districts for the manufacturing towns. And, augmenting this great supply of labor, came thousands of children—for an eight-year-old child was capable of operating a spinning-frame, in which, for this very reason, the spindles were set near to the floor. With an unlimited supply of labor, the cotton masters had only the cost of production to consider, and so it came about that they thought only of their profits and forgot the human hands which operated the machinery. England had fallen under the sway of a book—Adam Smith's *Wealth of Nations*, which, as Southey said, "considers man as a manufacturing animal, estimating his importance not by the goodness and knowledge he possesses, not by his virtues and charities, not by the happiness of which he may be the source and centre, not by the duties to which he is called, not by the immortal destinies for which he is created, but by the gain that may be extracted from him or of which he may be made the instrument."

The crowding of this vast laboring population into great industrial centres, however, gave rise to a class-consciousness which demanded that attention should be paid to the human element which distinguished labor from all other commodities, demanded that the cotton masters should no longer regard the workingman as a slave, or as merely a part of the machine, but as a free man, and which demanded further that this free man should be recognized as a citizen and given the right of suffrage.

It would be interesting for us to follow the history of the factory where we now leave it, firmly established as the cornerstone of Great Britain's wealth, down to the present time, and trace its development not only in England and America but throughout the civilized world. It is a surprising story of industrial progress, an important chapter in the social progress of mankind. But enough has already been said to prepare us for the consideration of the way in which the establishment of the factory affected England's laboring poor. The actual development of the cotton industry surpasses any dream that even the barber of Preston could have imagined when he exclaimed that he, unaided, would pay the national debt.

Less than a century and a half ago, Richard Arkwright built his first little mill at Nottingham which gave employment to a dozen operatives. To-day there are one hundred great cotton factories in the city of Fall River alone, operating three and one half million spindles, nearly one hundred thousand looms, and giving employment to twenty-seven thousand operatives. There are more than twenty-five million spindles in daily operation in the United States, and even a greater number on the continent of Europe, while Great Britain contains over fifty million; and when to these we add the spindles of India, Japan, and China, we have a total of one hundred and twenty million spindles giving employment to an army of workers as great as the entire population of England when Arkwright took out his patents for spinning by rollers. Nor is this all. The factory system first applied to the cotton industry has been applied to all manufactures as well as to agriculture and has become the central fact in modern industrial life.

We are now to take up the question of how the establishment of the factory affected England's laboring poor, and to study a little more in detail the social effects of the Industrial Revolution. In preparing the way for this discussion we should remember that the factory was not the sole cause of the Industrial Revolution, although it was a very important one. Other elements besides the introduction of machinery had gradually made possible production on a large scale. Chief among these was the decline of state regulation of industry, the development of rationalism quickening the scientific spirit, the growth of the empire and prestige of England which opened great export markets for the goods of British manufacture, the extension of banking facilities, and the construction of roads and canals. All these were elements in producing the Industrial Revolution. But what gave the movement force to revolutionize the social life of the common people was the factory, which gathered great masses of the population into industrial centres in which became possible the development of class consciousness.

V
THE FACTORY TOWNS

The dictionary contains the history of the race, if you search deep into its mysteries; every word tells its own story and bears its present meaning because men, at different times, thought precisely as they did and not otherwise.

Servius Tullius made six divisions of the citizens of Rome for the purposes of taxation and these divisions were called classes. A seventh included the mass of the population, those who were not possessed of any taxable property—that is to say the laboring poor. It is from this circumstance that our word "class" derives its peculiar meaning. Now it is significant that before the great extension of manufactures occasioned by the factory, we find no reference in our language to the working classes. The laboring poor belonged to no class; but when great cities grew up about the factories, populated by toilers whose interests in life were identical, the masses suddenly became conscious of their common life, their common needs, their common hopes. Blindly at first, and then more surely, they struggled for recognition as a class, and at last the struggle found expression in the language of their time. The arousing of this class consciousness amongst the workers I take to be the chief contribution of the factory to the social progress of mankind; and for this reason the rise of the manufacturing towns becomes a subject of great importance.

In the town hall at Manchester there is a fresco by Ford Maddox Brown which bears the title of "The Establishment of Flemish Weavers in Manchester," and shows Queen Philippa visiting the colony which she founded in 1363. Mr. George Saintsbury, in his history of Manchester, questions the historical accuracy of the event portrayed; "but," he adds, "Queen Philippa did many things which we should all be sorry to give up as art and literature and which, yet, are somewhat dubious history."

No one knows when Manchester first became a manufacturing town, and the introduction of Flemish artificers in the reign of Edward III is rather a probable than a certain starting-point. Nothing is distinctly known of the progress of woolen manufacture, until the reign of Henry VIII, at which time it had evidently grown into considerable importance. In the statute of the thirty-third year of his reign it appears that the inhabitants of Manchester carried on a considerable manufacture both of linens and woolens by which they were acquiring great wealth; but no mention has yet been found of cotton manufacture in that city earlier than the year 1641. By this time, however, it had become well established.

The labor was entirely handicraft; and it was not until the establishment of the factory by Arkwright that Manchester and the other manufacturing towns of England came into prominence in the political life of the nation; indeed it was not until the nineteenth century was well advanced that the inhabitants of these cities were represented in Parliament.

It has been held that the factory is an episode, not an element, in modern sociological development, and in a strict sense this is true. But because the factory led to the growth of great manufacturing towns and caused the migration thither of a vast population from the agricultural districts, and because it was among this population that the social discontent, which for a long period had existed in the lower classes, first became articulate, the factory directly contributed to the development of modern democracy.

The factory transformed not only craftsmen into operatives, but agricultural laborers as well, the latter becoming for the first time free to dispose of their own labor; for while serfdom had been declared illegal long before the establishment of the factory, yet the peasant remained dependent, in a large measure, upon the good will of his employer and he was bound by custom if not by law to the soil he tilled. The migration of this vast laboring population from the fields to the towns led to far-reaching social results.

"Meanwhile, at social Industry's command

How quick and fast an increase! From the germ

Of some poor hamlet, rapidly produced,

Here a large town, continuous and compact,

Hiding the face of earth for leagues—and there,

Where not a habitation stood before,

51

Abodes of men irregularly massed

Like trees in forests—spread through spacious tracts,

O'er which the smoke of unremitting fires

Hangs permanent, and plentiful as wreaths

Of vapor glittering in the morning sun."

Thus Wordsworth in *The Excursion* describes the rise of the manufacturing towns.

Our first concern is with the social conditions existing in these great manufacturing cities. The factory system was first applied to the spinning of yarn; but weaving continued, for a time, as a handicraft. This period was one of great prosperity to the hand-loom weavers. Before the invention of spinning-machinery, several spinners were required to furnish one loom with yarn; and one half of the weaver's time was spent in waiting for work. This time was employed in farming. But with the establishment of the spinning-mills the situation was reversed, and the weaver, plentifully supplied with yarn, ceased to cultivate the soil and devoted his whole time to the loom, a far more profitable occupation.

Villages of hand-loom weavers sprang up throughout the country adjacent to the manufacturing towns, and hither the master spinners sent their yarn and received back the finished cloth; while sometimes the weaving was done in "dandy" shops containing eight or ten and often as many as twenty looms. These little factories were usually owned by a single weaver who hired others to assist him in his work; but whatever the method, the profits from the business were always great.

"One of the happiest sights in Lancashire life at this time," writes a contemporary historian, "was the home of a family of weavers.... There could be heard the merry song to the tune of the clacking shuttles and the bumping of the lathes; the cottage surrounded with a garden filled with flowers and situated in the midst of green fields where the larks sang and the throstles whistled their morning adoration to the rising sun. The weaving thus carried on at home, where several persons of the same family and apprentices were employed, made them prosperous small manufacturers and a proud lot of people." This was about 1800.

"The trade of muslin weaver," says a Bolton manufacturer of the same period, "was that of a gentleman. The weavers brought home their work in top boots and ruffled shirts; they had a cane and took a coach in some instances, and appeared as well as military officers of the first degree. They used to walk about the streets with a five-pound Bank of England note spread out under their hat-bands; they would smoke none but long churchwarden pipes, and objected to the intrusion of any other craftsman into the particular rooms of the public-houses which they frequented." This abnormal prosperity, however, preceded their downfall. Two events were preparing it,—the invention of the power loom and the application of steam power to all the processes of manufacture.

Before considering the condition of the laboring population after the establishment of factories for weaving as well as for spinning, we should glance backward into the previous history of the laboring poor. During the prevalence of the feudal system the population of England was purely agricultural. The chief landed proprietors possessed a certain number of slaves who were employed generally in domestic service, but who also manufactured the wearing apparel and household furniture. "Priests are set apart for prayer," says an ancient chronicle, "but it is fit that noble chevaliers should enjoy all ease, and taste all pleasures, while the laborer toils, in order that they may be nourished in abundance—they, and their horse, and their dogs." This class of laborers, however, was never very large.

The great body of the peasantry was composed, first, of persons who rented small farms, and who paid their rent either in kind or in agricultural labor; and secondly, of cottagers, each of whom had a small parcel of land attached to his dwelling, and the privilege of turning out a cow, or pigs, or a few sheep into the woods, commons and wastes of the manor. During this whole period the entire population derived its subsistence immediately from the land. The mechanics of each village, not having time to cultivate a sufficient quantity of land to yield them a sustenance, received a fixed annual allowance of produce from each tenant. The peasantry worked hard and fared scantily enough, but still there was never an absolute want of food; the whole body was poor, but it contained no paupers.

During the fourteenth century the demand for wool not only to supply the markets of the Netherlands, but also the newly established manufacture of England, rapidly increased and the owners of the land found sheep-feeding more profitable than husbandry; and the sudden extension of manufacture in the fifteenth century greatly increased the demand. This circumstance led to an important change in the distribution of the population and the peasants previously employed in tillage were turned adrift upon the world. The allotments of arable land which had formerly afforded them the means of subsistence were converted into sheep walks and this policy greatly accelerated a social revolution which had already commenced. It eventually led to a complete severance between the English peasantry and the English soil; and with the exception of those employed in domestic manufacture, the little farmers and cottiers of the country were converted into day laborers depending entirely upon wages for their subsistence.

Thus when we come to consider the pitiable condition of the working classes, following the establishment of the factory, we must remember this underlying cause of the poverty and suffering, holding in mind the fact that from the beginning the increase of English poor rates kept pace visibly with the progress of the enclosure of the common land. Complaints against vagrancy and idleness, and the difficulty of providing for the poor increased proportionately with the progress of the system of consolidating farms, and abstracting from the English cottager his crofts and rights to the common lands. Upon the factory has fallen the blame for social conditions which had their source in causes long antedating its establishment—but the factory has sufficient misery for which to answer.

Arkwright's inventions, as we have seen, took manufactures out of the cottages and farm houses of England and assembled them in factories. Thousands of hands were suddenly required especially in Lancashire, which until then was comparatively thinly populated. A great migration of population from the rural districts to the manufacturing towns was set in motion, thousands of families leaving the quiet life of the country for the intenser life of the city, but still the new demand for labor was unsatisfied. The custom sprang up of procuring apprentices from the parish workhouses of London, Birmingham, and elsewhere; and many thousand children between the ages of seven and fourteen years were thus sent to swell the numbers of the laboring population. Beside the factories stood apprentice houses in which the children were lodged and fed; and it was also the custom for the master manufacturer to furnish the apprentice with clothes.

The work required of the children was exacting. The pay of the overseers was fixed in proportion to the work produced, a circumstance which bore hard on the apprentices. The greatest cruelties were practiced to spur the children to excessive labor; they were flogged, fettered, and in many cases they were starved and some were driven to commit suicide. We have it on the authority of Mr. John Fielding, himself, a master manufacturer and member of Parliament for Oldham, that the happiest moments in the lives of many of these children were those passed in the workhouse.

The profits of manufacturing were enormous and so was the greed of the newborn manufacturing aristocracy. Night work was begun, the day shift going to sleep in the same beds that the night shift had just quitted, so that it was a common saying in Lancashire that the beds never got cold. Although the master manufacturers were unmoved by the dictates of humanity, they were not proof against the malignant fevers which broke out in the congested districts and spread their ravages throughout the manufacturing towns.

Public opinion was soon aroused which led to the institution in Manchester of a board of health which in the year 1796 made an interesting report. It appeared that the children and others working in the cotton factories were peculiarly disposed to the contagion of fever; and that large factories were generally injurious to those employed in them even when no particular disease prevailed, not only on account of the close confinement and the debilitating effect of the hot and impure air, but on account of the untimely labor of the night and the protracted hours of the working day.

These conditions with respect to the children not only tended to diminish the sum of life by destroying the health and thus affecting the vital stamina of the rising generation; but it also encouraged idleness and profligacy in the parents, who, in many instances, lived upon the labor of their children. It further appeared that the children employed in factories were debarred from all opportunities of education as well as from moral and religious instruction. The investigation produced this report and nothing more— "when the dangers of infection were removed the precautions of mercy were forgotten."

Later, in the Parliamentary debate of 1815, Mr. Horner, one of the early factory reformers, graphically described the practices of the apprentice system. He told how, with a bankrupt's effects, a gang of workhouse children were put up for sale and publicly advertised as a part of the property; how a number of boys apprenticed by a parish in London to one manufacturer, had been transferred to another and in the process were left in a starving condition; how an agreement had been made between a London parish and a Lancashire manufacturer by which it was stipulated that with every twenty sound children one idiot should be taken.

Among the master manufacturers who had been incredulous concerning these conditions until the alarm of contagion arose, was the first Sir Robert Peel. He made a personal investigation and saw the abominations of the system; he declared his convictions and introduced into Parliament the first legislative measure for the protection of children. This was in the year 1802, and after many reverses he ultimately obtained the act known as the 42d Geo. III, "for the preservation of the Health and Morals of Apprentices and others, employed in Cotton and other mills."

This act is chiefly interesting because it established the principle of factory legislation, a principle which later in the century was greatly to promote the welfare of the masses. His first bill, however, referred only to apprentices and after its enactment children instead of being imported from the workhouses as formerly were nevertheless hired from their parents. Their services were dignified by the name of free labor, but because they were not accorded the protection given to apprentices their condition was little better than that of actual slavery.

The next step in the progress of factory legislation was to extend the protection to young persons engaged in manual employment whether apprentices or not. Time does not permit us to follow the interesting history of factory legislation, under the devoted leadership of Mr. Horner, Sir John Hobhouse (afterwards Lord Broughton), Mr. Saddler, and Lord Astley (afterwards the Earl of Shaftesbury). But the evidences of the social condition of the toilers brought out by the Parliamentary debates of 1816, 1818, 1819, and 1832, are all of the same nature and reveal a state of human misery without a parallel in history.

We turn now from child labor to the sanitary conditions of the manufacturing towns. The report printed by Doctor Kay in 1832, is an astounding document; it shows that out of six hundred and eighty-seven streets inspected, more than one half contained heaps of refuse or stagnant pools; and of nearly seven thousand houses inspected, more than one third were out of repair, damp, or ill-ventilated, and an equally large proportion lacked all sanitary conveniences, even of the most primitive kind.

The population lived on the simplest diet. Breakfast consisted of tea or coffee with a little bread, while sometimes the men had oatmeal porridge; dinner consisted generally of boiled potatoes heaped into one large dish over which melted lard was poured and sometimes a few pieces of fried fat bacon were added. Those who obtained higher wages or families whose aggregate income was large added a greater portion of animal food to this meal at least three times a week, but the quantity of meat consumed by the laboring population was not large.

The typical family sat around the table, plunging their spoons into the common dish and with animal eagerness satisfied the cravings of their appetite. The evening meal consisted of tea, often mingled with spirits and accompanied by a little bread. The population thus scantily nourished was crowded in one dense mass in cottages, separated by narrow, unpaved streets, in an atmosphere loaded with smoke. Engaged in an employment which unremittingly exhausted their physical energies, these men and women lacked every moral and intellectual stimulus; living in squalid wretchedness and on meagre food it was small wonder that their superfluous gains were spent in debauchery. With domestic economy neglected, domestic comfort unknown, home had no other relation to the factory operative than that of a shelter. At this period the number of operatives above the age of forty was incredibly small.

In a pamphlet printed during a great turnout in 1831, we find certain very interesting statistics concerning 1665 persons whose ages ranged between fifteen and sixty. Of these 1584 were under forty-five years of age, only fifty-one between forty-five and fifty were counted as fit for work, while only three had lived to be sixty years old. Such figures make it evident that large numbers of workers, prematurely unfitted for labor, came to live upon the toil of their own children. Nor was this all, for "puny and sickly parents gave birth to puny and sickly children, and thus the mischief continued its progress, one generation transmitting its accumulated evils to the next."

VI
CHARTISM

Such was the condition of the manufacturing population of England in the early days of the factory system. It is evident that these conditions must inevitably give rise to a deep social discontent which sooner or later must become articulate, and we find from the very beginning of the factory system the records of innumerable riots.

The history of these disturbances begins with the opposition to the introduction of new machinery. Rebellious craftsmen bound themselves by fearful oaths into secret organizations, the members of which were known as Luddites, from the name of their legendary leader—Ben Ludd. His name was the password to their secret meetings, at which plans were made for the destruction of property, plans afterwards carried out with open violence. Then followed innumerable riots arising from that growing social discontent which led in the beginning to factory legislation, and later to Parliamentary reform. It must not be thought that only the factory folk were discontented. The unrest was general throughout the lower classes; it was felt, moreover, in the ranks of the rapidly growing middle class, and the justice of the demand for better conditions was admitted now and then by individuals in the governing class—men of the broader vision. I have in my possession an interesting pamphlet containing the proceedings in the trial of indictment against Thomas Walker, a merchant of Manchester, and others, for a conspiracy to overthrow the constitution and government and to assist the French, the King's enemies, should they invade the Kingdom. The case was tried at the Assizes at Lancaster, in 1794, and the account throws light upon the true state of the public mind in Manchester at that time.

Thomas Walker, so it appeared to his accusers, was a pernicious, seditious, and ill-disposed person, greatly disaffected to the King, and who did in the hearing of divers liege subjects utter the words: "What are kings! Damn the King!" Moreover, Mr. Thomas Walker was a member of the Manchester Reformation Society, a body composed chiefly of working people. They met at a public house—the Old Boar's Head, where the works of Tom Paine were read aloud over innumerable pots of ale; and a correspondence was carried on with the Society of the Friends of the People in London and with other more questionable organizations. The publican, warned by the magistrates that he must no longer give entertainment to this society, turned the reformers into the streets, whereupon they sought shelter in the warehouse of Mr. Walker. Here it was alleged they were trained in the use of firearms; and here one night they were attacked by members of the Church and King Club, and a riot ensued. The Reformation Society, however, maintained that the sole object of their meetings was to obtain, by constitutional means, an adequate representation of the people in Parliament.

Discontent continues rife in Manchester, increasing with each year, and at last we come to an event which typifies to all time this upward struggle of toiling humanity—the massacre on St. Peter's Field which occurred on the 16th of August, 1819. Throughout the whole preceding summer, on account of the distressed condition of trade, discontent had been rife in the manufacturing towns; agitation was at white heat; and the voice of the demagogue was heard with that of the conscientious reformer. It was proposed to hold at Manchester on the 9th of August an immense meeting to consider the election by the unrepresented inhabitants of Manchester of a Parliamentary delegate; but the purpose of this meeting was declared illegal and it was prohibited by the authorities. Then another meeting was advertised to take place on the 16th of August, the stated object being to consider the most legal and effectual means of obtaining Parliamentary reform. It was said that this meeting was attended by over one hundred thousand persons.

Several of the divisions that composed the assembly came upon the field in regular military formations, accompanied by bands of music and preceded by banners bearing such mottoes as "Equal Representation or Death." Many of the marchers were armed with bludgeons. Most of the columns, however, marched in silence; and except for the loud shouts of defiance on the appearance of the yeomen cavalry, sent to disperse the meeting, there was no disturbance on the part of the populace.

The assembly was in charge of Henry Hunt, the famous radical, who, mounting the platform which had been erected upon a cart had just commenced his opening speech when the civil authorities attempted to arrest him. This the mob resisted, whereupon the yeoman cavalry shouting, "Have down with their banners!" charged upon the field, put the crowds to flight, and in the disorder which followed, a number were killed and many were wounded.

Says Carlyle: "Who shall compute the waste and loss, the obstruction of every sort, that was produced in the Manchester region by Peterloo alone. Some thirteen unarmed men and women cut down—the number of the slain and maimed is very countable; but the treasury of rage, burning hidden or visible in all hearts ever since, is of unknown extent. 'How ye came among us, in your cruel armed blindness, ye unspeakable County Yeomanry, sabres flourishing, hoofs prancing, and slashed us down at your brute pleasure; deaf, blind to all our claims, and woes and wrongs; of quick sight and sense to your own claims only. There lie poor sallow, workworn weavers, and complain no more now; women themselves are slashed and sabred, howling terror fills the air; and ye ride prosperous, very victorious,—ye unspeakable: Give us sabres too and then come on a little!'"

The treasury of rage burning hidden became visible to all. Chartism—the demand of the people for equal political rights—sprang into being; the outward and visible sign of inward suppressed discontent filled the manufacturing towns with unrestrained murmurings, and government felt the castle of privilege trembling at its foundation. Some days later Sidmouth, writing from Whitehall, congratulated the yeomanry in the name of the Prince Regent for their effective services in preserving public tranquillity. Public tranquillity indeed! The cries of those stricken weavers shall yet shake the empire of Britain.

Peterloo was typical of the discontent which had spread throughout the laboring population of England. Parliament was assembled in special session to consider the state of the country and to enact measures for the suppression of disorder. Lord Grenfell in a brilliant speech discussed sedition, declaring that the whole nation was inundated with inflammatory publications intended to stimulate the multitude to acts of savage violence against all who were eminent for birth or rank, for talent or virtue. Mr. Canning placed the blame entirely upon discontented radicals, underrating the wide-spread demand for parliamentary reform, and advocated the acts which were passed prohibiting meetings like the one held in Manchester, and in other ways restricting the liberties of the masses in discussing social conditions. All of these acts tended to increase the discontent and hasten forward that reform which alone could save England from revolution.

All famous Englishmen, however, did not view Peterloo with the eyes of Lord Grenfell or Mr. Canning. Writing to Thomas Love Peacock, Shelley said: "Many thanks for your attention in sending the papers which contained the terrible and important news of Manchester. These are, as it were, the distant thunders of the terrible storm which is approaching. The tyrants here, as in the French Revolution, have first shed blood. May their execrable lessons not be learnt with equal docility." Inspired by the Manchester massacre, Shelley wrote "The Masque of Anarchy," the spirit of which is summed up in these stanzas:—

"Men of England, heirs of Glory,

Heroes of unwritten story,

Nurselings of one mighty Mother,

Hopes of her, and one another;

"Rise like Lions after slumber

In unvanquishable number,

Shake your chains to earth like dew

Which in sleep has fallen on you—

Ye are many—they are few."

And in the same year he wrote:—

"Men of England, wherefore plough

For the Lords who lay ye low?

Wherefore weave with toil and care

The rich robes your tyrants wear?

"Wherefore feed, and clothe, and save,

From the cradle to the grave,

Those ungrateful drones who would

Drain your sweat—nay, drink your blood?

"The seed ye sow, another reaps;

The wealth ye find, another keeps;

The robes ye weave, another wears;

The arms ye forge, another bears.

"Sow seed,—but let no tyrant reap;

Find wealth,—let no impostor heap;

Weave robes,—let not the idle wear;

Forge arms,—in your defense to bear."

Fortunately the appeal to arms was unnecessary. The working classes of England were destined to exemplify Shelley's lesson,—but by peaceful means,—were destined to teach the world the great truth that the many, if accordant and resolute, can always control the few. And this peaceful conquest is recorded in the history of Chartism.

I have known many labor agitators living in the City of the Dinner Pail, and almost without exception these men were the sons of English Chartists. From them I had learned to honor the early British labor agitator, and to give to the name of pothouse politician something more than a contemptuous meaning. At the Old Boar's Head, in Manchester, and at many another less famous public house in the manufacturing cities, groups of workingmen gathered, evening after evening to discuss their wrongs; and over many a pot of ale, and through many a cloud of tobacco smoke, there emerged at last certain definite demands for reform.

Workingmen and radicals joined hands; liberal leaders combined with working-class leaders, and presently there was issued the famous Charter with its six points,— manhood suffrage, annual parliaments, the ballot, abolition of property qualifications, payment of members, and equality of electoral districts. A very sober programme this, but popular leaders like Fergus O'Connor and Ernest Jones with incendiary oratory gave it a revolutionary aspect.

So the discontent grew year by year, and year by year it gathered force. Events in France and elsewhere on the continent excited the imagination of the governing classes, and every meeting place of workingmen appeared to be bristling with firearms, but still the movement grew, and at last the workingmen were ready with their petition to Parliament. When, on the morning of the 10th of April, 1848, bands of Chartists began to gather on Kennington Common, carrying red banners and tricolors, all London was astir with excitement. Government had taken precaution for its defense; the guns of the Tower were manned and loaded; the employees of the post-office were supplied with two thousand rifles; the bank was surrounded with artillery; and behind sand-bags piled upon its roof stood a regiment of infantry. The bridges and approaches to Westminster were defended by an army of ten thousand horse, foot, and artillery, while the six thousand police of London lined the streets, supported by an army of special constables. And in command of this elaborate defense of the city against four thousand unarmed workingmen assembled on Kennington Common to bear a petition to Parliament, was none other than the Iron Duke himself—Wellington. Surely the voice of the pothouse politicians had been heard throughout England; it had penetrated the halls of government—what need had the reformers for powder and shot? And must we not believe that when five years later the great reform was enacted, credit for that event was in some measure due to the resolute and accordant factory folk? Yes, the wheels and spindles of which Arkwright dreamed brought something more than material wealth to England; his vision made the nation rich and powerful and his vision likewise gave to the masses equal political rights.

VII
THE FACTORY AND SOCIAL PROGRESS

We have now traced the history of the factory, from its beginning with the inventions of Arkwright down to its permanent establishment in the first half of the last century, and we have noted its influence upon the social life of England. We have seen how, as early as the fifteenth century, the introduction of manufactures assisted in breaking down the feudal system, and how, by making possible the accumulation of wealth by men of humble birth, it contributed to the rise of the middle class. We have further seen that at the close of the eighteenth century the introduction of machinery intensified these tendencies and exerted a powerful influence on the development of our modern democracy.

We have, however, confined our attention to a single industry as it developed in a particular nation,—we have taken the cotton factory as typical of all factories and its growth in England as typical of its growth throughout the Western world. But the factory has developed differently in each industry and its social influence has never been quite alike in any two nations. When, for instance, Samuel Slater introduced cotton manufacturing into America, he set up in Rhode Island an exact counterpart of the English factory. When, later, other factories were built in New England there took place the same transition of a vast laboring population from the rural districts to the manufacturing towns;—but this population was very unlike the manufacturing population of England. The American factories were operated by the sons and daughters of Yankee farmers, reared in the atmosphere of democracy and springing from a race unaffected by the traditions of feudalism; for them political equality had been already won, yet even in America the factory became an instrument for social progress. In the rapidly growing manufacturing towns these country folk found a new life of opportunity for social advancement; they did not remain operatives long, but advanced to higher callings; and to take the places which they left, thousands of workers came from Lancashire here to enjoy that civic freedom for which their brothers in the Old World were still contending. To-day in our Southern States we see a similar process at work,—another race of men advancing in the social scale by means of the factory; from the mountains of the Carolinas thousands of young men and women, reared in a civilization almost unbelievably primitive, are flocking to the manufacturing towns, there to enjoy the advantages of modern life. But however varied have been the phases of the development of the factory in different parts of the world there has always been this common phenomenon—the concentration of the laboring population in manufacturing cities and the development of social discontent leading to social progress.

The nineteenth century was the age of Power Discovered; mechanical inventions, the concentration of industry, the extension of the factory system, new means of transportation destroyed the last vestige of the feudal world and left the democratic ideal triumphant but unfulfilled: a new century dawns,—the age of Power Humanized. The industrial world in which we live, with all its peculiar characteristics, has been built upon the ruins of the feudal order, and in due time will give place to a newer and better civilization. Radicals of to-day see visions of to-morrow; reformers fired by the visions seek to make them real; while conservatives, clinging to the traditions of a dead past, strive to stay the inevitable progress of mankind. Truth never changes, but the knowledge of truth grows deeper with each age; no political institution, no social institution is sacred unless it is founded upon some eternal truth, and all human institutions must change with the increasing knowledge of mankind. Everywhere in the Western world the condition of the laboring population is vastly better to-day than when, a century and a half ago, the factory was established; vastly better than when, sixty years ago, the governments of Europe trembled before a working-class revolt,—when British Chartism triumphed in reform; when Karl Marx, exiled from Prussia, called upon the workingmen of the world to unite; when Mazzini, another exile in London, preached to the toilers of Italy the gospel of God and humanity, of progress through education. But the evolution is incomplete, and the discontent of the laboring population still remains a vital force in the upward progress of mankind.

To-day we in America are confronted by the amazing spread of Socialism; Socialism which the radicals preach, the reformers seek to establish, and the conservatives fear. We cannot evade its issues, for Socialism is something more than a political creed,—it is the modern expression of that same spirit of human progress which destroyed slavery in the ancient world, serfdom in the middle ages and, creating modern democracy, cannot rest until it has guaranteed to all men not only equal political rights but equal social rights. Two men, smoke-room companions of mine during a Pacific voyage, stand for the contending ideals of the feudal and the modern world. One was a noble earl, the other a British tea merchant; both were men of wealth,—the one of large but unproductive estates, the other of a great business giving employment to thousands of men. Of the two, the tea merchant, though lacking in fine manners, was the more important person; yet he would not have exchanged those hours of familiar gossip with the noble earl for more chests of tea than would fill the hold of the ship. And there was a reason for this feeling, because the Groom of the Bedchamber stood for that aristocracy of culture and good manners which has an important value in any society. Under the militant structure of society this value belonged to the few; in our present democracy it has become increasingly the privilege of the many. Public education, public libraries, public art galleries, the perfected art of printing have opened the highest culture to children of the humblest birth. May we not, then, look forward to the time when "the best that has anywhere been in the world shall be the lot of every man born into it"—that is to say, the lot of every man who desires the best?

Every thinking man must admit that there is something wrong in our present industrial régime. The progress of avowed Socialism and the more rapid progress of particular socialistic ideas indicate quite clearly that we Americans are alive to the unequal social conditions which now exist and are anxious to find a remedy. But whatever may be the utopian dreams of the reformers, all immediate progress must be made in the industrial world as we find it to-day; the industrial state of the Socialist is too remote in time,—our task is with social conditions as they now exist. The splendid machinery of production created during the last century must not be destroyed, but utilized for the benefit of mankind. The question which we have now to ask ourselves is this: What is the ultimate purpose for which the business of the world is conducted, what the real purpose of all this planting and reaping, this mining and manufacturing, this exchanging of commodities? Is it not, primarily, to furnish each human creature with food, shelter, and clothing,—the means of supporting life? Men require something more than the mere means of subsistence; but before the individual can cultivate his mind and soul his body must be made comfortable, and this, after all, is the whole end of our complex commercial régime. The test of right and wrong conduct in business refers to this fundamental purpose,—that conduct only is praiseworthy which advances the time when every man capable of industry shall be rewarded for his labor, not only with a loaf of bread, but with hours of fruitful leisure.

Captains of Industry! that was a noble title Carlyle gave to the prosaic business man, when gazing beyond the squalid turmoil of his day with its dominant industrialism, triumphant mercantilism, doctrines of *laissez-faire*, overproduction, surplus population, he with clear vision foresaw the future freedom of the masses won through their own strength and the ability of their leaders. Until Richard Arkwright was born, the leaders of men in their progress towards human freedom had been soldiers; henceforward they were to be men of affairs. Great soldiers won their victory by the loyalty they inspired in their followers; no adventurer seeking personal glory ever won a lasting victory, but only those heroes, forgetful of themselves who consecrated their service to the cause of freedom. In such wise must Captains of Industry win their victories; the adventurer can but for a time prevail; fame is secure only to those leaders who see in wealth accumulated a treasure held in trust from which they are to feed and clothe the armies that they lead to peaceful conquests. Social reformers of sentimental temper have deemed the comparison between the modern employer of labor and the feudal lord as ill-chosen, but history seems to justify it. Yet we have, indeed, gone far since the Middle Ages. When the feudal lord demanded loyalty from his retainers the demand was alone sufficient, but the Captain of Industry, in order to obtain the loyalty of the toilers, must not only demand but deserve it; he too must be loyal to the great cause he serves—the eternal cause of human freedom.

THE END

CONTENTS